Dear Parent:
Your child's love of reading starts here!

W9-BNZ-797

Every child learns to read in a different way and at his or her own speed. Some go back and forth between reading levels and read favorite books again and again. Others read through each level in order. You can help your young reader improve and become more confident by encouraging his or her own interests and abilities. From books your child reads with you to the first books he or she reads alone, there are I Can Read Books for every stage of reading:

SHARED READING
Basic language, word repetition, and whimsical illustrations, ideal for sharing with your emergent reader

BEGINNING READING
Short sentences, familiar words, and simple concepts for children eager to read on their own

READING WITH HELP
Engaging stories, longer sentences, and language play for developing readers

READING ALONE
Complex plots, challenging vocabulary, and high-interest topics for the independent reader

I Can Read Books have introduced children to the joy of reading since 1957. Featuring award-winning authors and illustrators and a fabulous cast of beloved characters, I Can Read Books set the standard for beginning readers.

A lifetime of discovery begins with the magical words **"I Can Read!"**

Visit www.icanread.com for information on enriching your child's reading experience.

I Can Read® and I Can Read Book® are trademarks of HarperCollins Publishers.

Danny and the Dinosaur Ride a Bike
Copyright © 2020 by The Authors Guild Foundation, Anti-Defamation League Foundation, ORT America, Inc., and United Negro College Fund, Inc.
All rights reserved. Printed in the United States of America.
No part of this book may be used or reproduced in any manner whatsoever without written permission except in the case of brief quotations embodied in critical articles and reviews. For information address HarperCollins Children's Books, a division of HarperCollins Publishers, 195 Broadway, New York, NY 10007.
www.icanread.com

Library of Congress Control Number: 2019944389
ISBN 978-0-06-285761-3 (trade bdg.)—ISBN 978-0-06-241055-9 (pbk.)

Book design by Rick Farley

23 24 SCP 10 9 8 7   ❖   First Edition

I Can Read!

Syd Hoff's
DANNY AND THE DINOSAUR

Ride a Bike

Written by Bruce Hale
Illustrated in the style of Syd Hoff
by Charles Grosvenor

HARPER
An Imprint of HarperCollinsPublishers

One day, when Danny went to visit

his friend the dinosaur,

the two friends saw a huge bicycle

in front of the museum.

"Wow!" said the dinosaur.

"I wonder what that's for?"

5

"There's a new exhibit," said Danny, "all about the history of bicycles."

"That sounds like fun,"

said the dinosaur.

"So why do you look sad?"

7

Danny frowned. "I can't ride a bike.
Betty can ride, Sofia can ride,
even Zig-Zag Zack can ride.

But not me," he said.

"If they can learn, you can learn,"
said the dinosaur.

"I don't know. . ." said Danny.

"Come on," said the dinosaur.

"It'll be easy.

I'll help you."

They borrowed Betty's bicycle.

The dinosaur put lots of pillows
around the parking lot to give
Danny a soft landing.

But it didn't work the way
the dinosaur planned.

13

Each time Danny fell off,

he totally missed the pillows!

OUCH!

"Sorry!" said the dinosaur.

"Balancing is tricky," said Danny.

"You're thinking too much,"
said the dinosaur.
"Here, I'll distract you.
Let's sing a song."

"Row, row, row your boat,"

sang Danny.

"Gently down the—whoa!"

Danny tumbled off again.

"This is too hard," he said.

"I should just quit."

"Nonsense," said the dinosaur.

"We'll try again tomorrow!"

The next day, the dinosaur lay down
in the parking lot.
"Just ride along beside my tail,"
he said.

"That way, you can lean on me
if you're about to fall."

21

Danny gave it a try.

But instead of leaning

on his friend's tail,

he ran it over—yikes!

22

And Danny fell again—ouch!

"This really isn't working,"
said Danny.
"Maybe some people
just can't ride bikes."

The dinosaur didn't know what to do.

How could he help his friend?

When Danny walked the bike away,

he almost stepped on a mouse!

Danny was so surprised,

he jumped into his bicycle seat.

The bike rolled gently downhill,
and Danny didn't fall!

Danny put his feet on the pedals.

And just like that, he was riding!

"I'm doing it!" he whooped.

"I'm riding a bike!"

The dinosaur cheered, "Yay, Danny!
I knew you could do it!"

"I wish we could ride together,"
said Danny.

The dinosaur smiled. "Maybe we can."

"What do you mean?" asked Danny.

The dinosaur brought out the big bike

from the museum.

"I've been practicing," he said.

"But I didn't want to tell you

until you could ride too."

"What are we waiting for?"
said Danny.
"Let's ride!"